The Saddest Toilet in the World

By
SAM APPLE

Illustrated by
SAM RICKS

Aladdin

NEW YORK   LONDON   TORONTO   SYDNEY   NEW DELHI

To Isaiah, who potty trained during the creation of this book —S. R.

ALADDIN / An imprint of Simon & Schuster Children's Publishing Division / 1230 Avenue of the Americas, New York, New York 10020 / First Aladdin hardcover edition June 2016 / Text copyright © 2016 by Sam Apple / Illustrations copyright © 2016 by Sam Ricks / All rights reserved, including the right of reproduction in whole or in part in any form. / ALADDIN is a trademark of Simon & Schuster, Inc., and related logo is a registered trademark of Simon & Schuster, Inc. / For information about special discounts for bulk purchases, please contact Simon & Schuster Special Sales at 1-866-506-1949 or business@simonandschuster.com. / The Simon & Schuster Speakers Bureau can bring authors to your live event. For more information or to book an event contact the Simon & Schuster Speakers Bureau at 1-866-248-3049 or visit our website at www.simonspeakers.com. / Book designed by Karin Paprocki / The illustrations for this book were rendered with a brush pen, watercolors, and then digitally combined. / The text of this book was set in Family Dog Fat. / Manufactured in China 0316 SCP / 2 4 6 8 10 9 7 5 3 1 / Library of Congress Control Number 2015956695 / ISBN 978-1-4814-5122-2 (hc) / ISBN 978-1-4814-5123-9 (eBook)

Danny loved sitting on the floor.

He could sit on the couch all day.

The beanbag was his favorite seat of all.

But there was one place Danny did not want to sit.

"Just try," Mom said.

"I'm not sure," Danny said.

I'll give you a special treat.

Danny thought about it.
"I'm just not ready."

"I don't understand. What does the couch have that I don't?"

"Danny is just a little, well . . . scared of you."

"Scared of me? But I'm so nice."

"I think you're wonderful," Danny's mom said. "I'm sure Danny will want to sit on you soon."

"I simply can't go on like this," the toilet said.
"It's just too hurtful."

Danny's mom tried to make the toilet feel better.

But the toilet had made his decision. That night he packed his things . . .

and left.

But the toilet had made
his decision. That night he
packed his things . . .

and left.

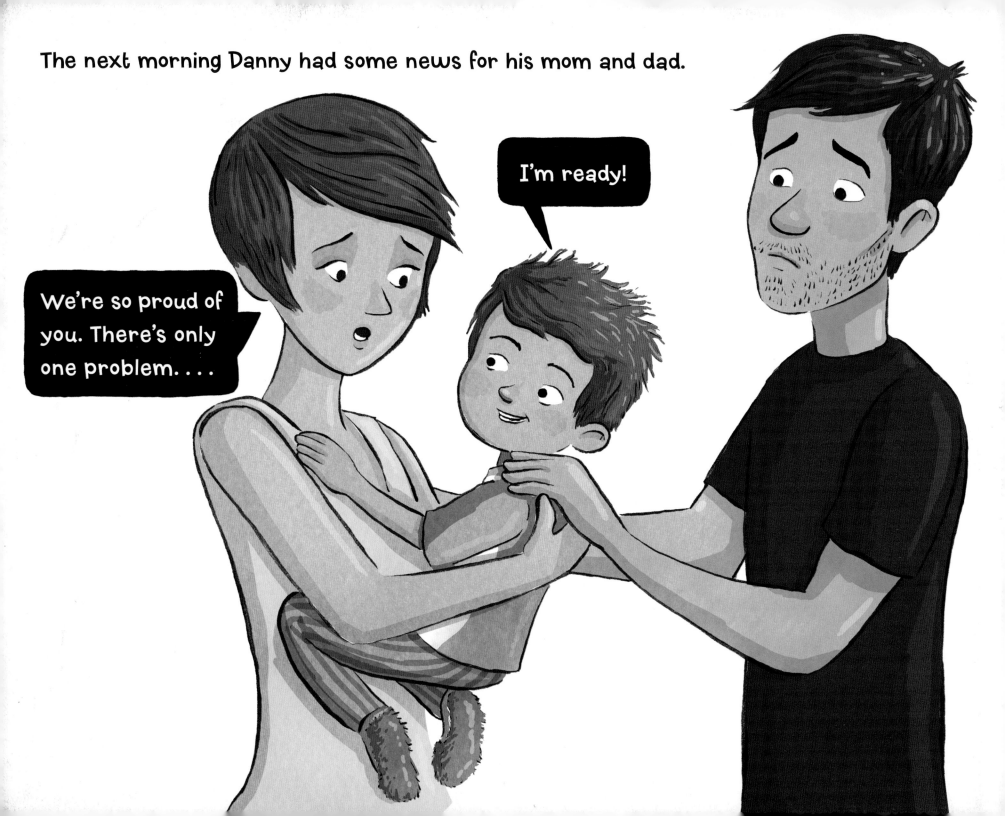

They looked everywhere.

But in all the wrong places.

Danny and his mom were almost ready to give up,

until Danny spotted something.

They ran as fast as they could. But the toilet was gone.

"I don't want a new toilet," Danny said.
"I want . . . Mom! Look!"

"This is my stop," the toilet said.

"Wait!"
Danny called.

"Thank you," the toilet said. "Is that all?"

"No," Danny answered.

"No, that's not all."

"What I want to tell you is that . . ."
Danny took a deep breath.

"What I want to tell you is that . . . I'm ready! I'm ready to sit on you!"

"And you really mean it?" the toilet asked. "You're not just saying that?"

"Come back home," Danny said. "I'll show you."

The toilet returned to Danny's bathroom. And Danny showed the toilet he WAS ready.

"I've never felt so happy!" the toilet said.

"This calls for a celebration," the toilet said.